Martha Camps Out

Adaptation by Karen Barss

Based on a TV series teleplay written by Melissa Stephenson and Raye Lankford

Based on the characters created by Susan Meddaugh

HOUGHTON MIFFLIN HARCOURT
Boston • New York

Ages 5–7 | Grade: 2 | Guided Reading Level: K | Reading Recovery Level: 18

Copyright © 2011 WGBH Educational Foundation and Susan Meddaugh.
"MARTHA" and all characters and underlying materials (including artwork) from the "MARTHA" books are trademarks of
and copyrights of Susan Meddaugh and used under license. All other characters and underlying materials are trademarks of and
copyrights of WGBH. All rights reserved. The PBS KIDS logo is a registered mark of PBS and is used with permission.

For information about permission to reproduce selections from this book,
write to Permissions, Houghton Mifflin Harcourt Publishing Company,
215 Park Avenue South, New York, New York 10003.

Library of Congress Cataloging-in-Publication Data is on file.
ISBN 978-0-547-55619-2 pb | ISBN 978-0-547-55618-5 hc
Design by Rachel Newborn
www.hmhbooks.com | www.marthathetalkingdog.com

Manufactured in Singapore | TWP 10 9 8 7 6 5 4 3 2
4500273809

Alice and Helen are Junior Gophers.
Mrs. Clusky is their group leader.
She is taking the two girls camping.

Mrs. Clusky says, "Alice and Helen want to earn merit badges."
"Good luck!" the group says.

Alice and Helen pack for the trip.
They are going to Flea Island.
"I love the outdoors," says Alice.
"This is going to be so much fun!"

But Alice's brother does not agree.
"You guys are *going camping?*" Ronald asks.
"I would not camp with Big Minnie around."

Big Minnie?

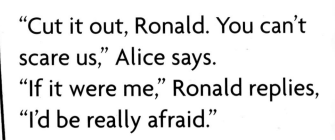

"Cut it out, Ronald. You can't scare us," Alice says.
"If it were me," Ronald replies, "I'd be really afraid."

"Who's Big Minnie?" Martha asks.
"Oh, just some monster," Alice says.
"MONSTER!" Martha cries.
"There's no such thing as monsters,"
Helen says.

Ronald bikes off.
"Ronald, wait!" calls Martha.
"Tell me about Big Minnie."
Ronald stops. "Some say she isn't real,
but she is."

"She only comes out at night,"
Ronald says.
He uses a spooky voice.
"When the moon is full, she howls like this:

Aaawwwhhhooooooooooooo."

That night, Martha is worried.
"If you are going camping," she says
to Helen, "I am going with you.
I have to protect you!"

Thanks, Martha!

The next morning is sunny and clear.
The girls, Mrs. Clusky, and the dogs paddle
to Flea Island.

They work together to set up camp.
They eat around the campfire.

They prepare for bed.
No monsters lurking here!

Everybody is asleep except Martha and Skits.
They guard the tents.
"No sign of Big Minnie," Martha says.
"I guess we can go to bed."
But just then—

AAAWW

Martha and Skits jump into the tent.
"It's Big Minnie!" Martha yelps.
"Ronald did her howl for me, just like that!"

Alice stands up.
"Wait a minute.
Ronald howled
just like that?"

Ronald hides in the woods.
He laughs as he plays his recording.

Then he hears something in
the bushes. What is it?
"Oh, no! It's Big Minnie! She's real!"
he shouts.

Ronald panics. He runs away.
The girls watch him jump into the
lake and swim home.

"That will show him," Alice says, laughing.
"Now let's go back to bed."

Back in the tent, a sound wakes Martha.
She peeks outside.
"Hey," Martha whispers, "keep it down—!"
She looks up. Way up.

But Big Minnie purrs softly.
And Martha smiles.
"Hello, Big Minnie," she says,
quietly. "Don't worry.
Your secret is safe with me."

"I won't tell anyone you are real," says Martha. "I promise."